Pigsty

by MARK TEAGUE

SCHOLASTIC
HARDCOVER

SCHOLASTIC INC.

New York

 onday afternoon Wendell Fultz's mother told him to clean his room. "It's turning into a pigsty," she said.

Wendell went upstairs. Much to his surprise,
a large pig was sitting on his bed.

"Pardon me," said Wendell. He shoved some toys into his closet. But the pig didn't seem to mind the mess, and Wendell found that he didn't mind the pig, either.

He decided to take a break.

When Wendell's mother came to look
at his room, the pig was hiding, but the mess
was still there. She threw up her hands.

"Okay, Wendell," she said. "If you want
to live in a pigsty, that's up to you."

Wendell could hardly believe his luck. "Now I can live however I want."

He didn't even worry when he came home on Tuesday and found a second pig in his room. The mess had grown a bit worse, but he was able to jam most of it under his bed.

"Pigs are all right," he said, "as long as it's only one or two."

In fact, they had a wonderful time. They played Monopoly until late each night . . .

. . . and left the pieces lying all over the floor.

They had paper airplane wars and pillow fights.

The bed became a trampoline.

Then two more pigs showed up.
The mess just grew and grew.

That night when Wendell went to bed, the pigs
were lying everywhere. They rolled up in his blankets
and hogged his pillows, too.

Wendell told himself he didn't mind,
but then he found hoofprints on his
comic books.

And Friday when he got home from school, he saw that someone had been sitting on his basketball.

And his baseball cards were chewed.

"That does it!" said Wendell. "I've had enough!"
He ran downstairs to tell his mother.

"Sorry," she said, "but your room is your responsibility." She handed him a broom.

Wendell started to complain. The mess was too huge. But suddenly he remembered a saying he'd heard, that "many hooves make light work."

He marched upstairs and organized a cleaning crew.

They swept and scoured, polished and scrubbed.

Later that afternoon, Wendell inspected his room
and pronounced it "clean."

In fact, it was a bit too clean, from a pig's point of view. So while Wendell inspected, the pigs prepared to go home. One of them made a phone call, and a farm truck came to pick them up. They hugged and grunted and oinked "good-bye."

From that day on, Wendell kept his room clean . . .

. . . except for those nights when his friends came by to play Monopoly.

For Bill and Becky,
Katherine, Christopher and Alanna

Library of Congress Cataloging-in-Publication Data

Teague, Mark.
Pigsty / by Mark Teague.
p.   cm.
Summary: When Wendell doesn't clean up his room, a whole herd of
pigs comes to live with him.
ISBN 0-590-45915-5
[1. Pigs — Fiction. 2. Cleanliness — Fiction. 3. Orderliness —
Fiction.] I. Title. II. Title: Pigsty.
PZ7.T2193825Pi 1994
[E] — dc20   93-21179
CIP
AC

20 19 18 17 16   0/2
Printed in the U.S.A.   37

First printing, September 1994

The illustrations in this book were painted in acrylic.

Book design by David Turner